Aron and the Police Give Back to the Community

Introduction

As a children's author and former civic leader, I have focused on bringing people together, doing whatever I can to foster connections between others and empower them to understand each other. This is almost never easy work, but the more that I do it and the more I commit myself to it, the more that it seems to repay me. It is always fulfilling to see that I have made a difference in a person's life, especially a young person.

Towards that end, this children's book will examine and discuss police and community relations in a way that is lighthearted, fun, and clear. I want this book to become a go-to resource for organizations and police departments striving to work toward positive change.

-Nahjee

In a small neighborhood in Philadelphia, there was a young boy named Aron, who would soon find himself on a mission to better his community.

Recent events show a rise in tension between law enforcement and local community members.

As Aron played, the stories of protests played on the television.

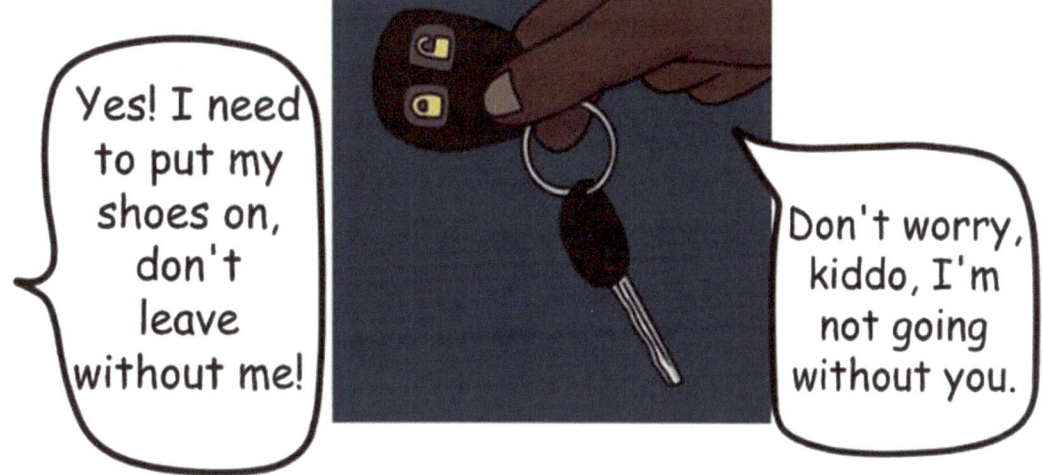

Aron went with his father to the supermarket in the hopes of getting his favorite snacks.

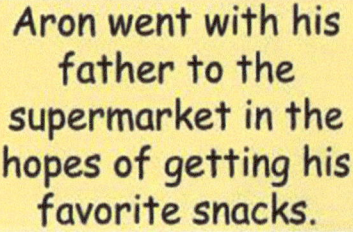

Dad, can I get a bag of cookies?

Sure, kiddo, but only if you promise to share.

I promise!

Aron helped his father get groceries for their home, never forgetting to grab a bag of cookies.

Okay!

Alright, I think that's enough groceries for today. Let's go.

Something caught Aron's attention, for he noticed the presence of police made everyone around sad or angry.

8

Son, you know that there are bad people and there are good people in the world, right?

Yeah.

Well, sometimes bad people take spots that are supposed to be good and abuse that position. Understand?

Are there still good people in those spots?

Of course there are! But it's easier to notice the bad things in life than the good ones.

Oh. Okay, that makes sense.

9

It was then that Aron promised to help his community.

Then I'll help everyone see the good first!

Determined, Aron set his first sights on his best friends, recruiting them for his goal to better their community.

I'm going to help all our friends and family in the community. You've gotta help me!

Well, what do we have to do?

Caught up in his excitement, Aron realized he still didn't have any ideas on how to achieve his goals.

Inspired by his determination, Mindy, Dave, Barbara joined Aron's team and they all worked hard to make plans for their community.

Ready for the day of his meeting, Aron did his best to dress to impress.

Here, let me help you.

Thanks, Dad!

Ready for his big meeting, Aron and Dad made the trip to the local police station.

You ready, kiddo?

Yeah!

Ready to achieve his goals, Aron took the lead and spoke up first.

13

14

Ready for the next stage of his goal, Aron pitched the ideas he and Barbara, Ali, Dave came up with and designed sample flyers.

My team and I made sample signs for ideas we have to help the community better their relationship with police.

These are great ideas, Aron! Do you have a specific one in mind that you want to do first?

A week later, Aron and his friends received word on their plans for the toy drive.

Okay, Alison, thank you for calling... That's right, I'll tell them. Bye.

Well? What happened? What did she say?

Did they like our ideas?

That was Alison just now. She wanted to call us herself and tell us their entire station wants to participate in the toy drive that will be happening in one month.

We did it!

Hi, JoAnn! We're helping with a toy drive that the police will be participating in.

A toy drive?

Yeah! We'll get to meet a policeman or police woman and we get an awesome free toy!

Soon, all the kids in the neighborhood got news of the toy drive.

Mommy, mommy, can we go?

Together with the team at the police station, Aron and his friends were able to help run a toy drive that all the neighborhood showed up to.

Don't be nervous, here, how would you like this?

20

It was a day of smiles and laughter, and Aron was proud to see his neighborhood there.

Your Idea was a success, Aron!

I'm really proud of you, son.

21

Ready for the next part of his plan to better his community relations, Aron wanted to pursue his next event.

So, Aron, what's next for you?

There's so much still left to do! I'm going to do everything to help my community

Inspired by his determination, more neighborhood children soon joined Aron in his goals of helping better their community.

Okay, Dad and I went with Alison to the library yesterday and they agreed to hosting a book drive there in a month.

Oh, oh! We can ask the neighborhood if they have books they want to donate

Aron and his friends planted a garden for Social Justice & Peace. They plan on building future gardens throughout the community.

With a loving heart and caring soul, Aron continued to follow through and help his community. His dad always right by his side cheering him on.

Aron became known as a local leader for his community service, often being interviewed by the news station.

Thank You Sponsors!

This book was made possible by a successful crowdfunding campaign and the following top supporters are noted and appreciated:

Sherimane Johnson
Jen Crompton
Sarah Altman
Ardmore Toyota
David M. Perry
Barbara J. Spencer
Allison Anmuth
Jackie McLean
Ali Daniel
Amy McCann
Mindy Cohen
Mike and Roseann Mcgrath

Police2Peace is a proud supporter of Aron and the Police Give Back to The Community for the way it unites police departments and communities to uplift and heal them.

www.ingramcontent.com/pod-product-compliance
Lightning Source LLC
Chambersburg PA
CBHW041543240626
47164CB00002B/114